Litte Girl Lost

Daddies' Lost Girls, Volume 1

Rose Nickol

Published by Rose Nickol, 2024.

This is a work of fiction. Similarities to real people, places, or events are entirely coincidental.

LITTE GIRL LOST

First edition. October 24, 2024.

Copyright © 2024 Rose Nickol.

ISBN: 979-8227624567

Written by Rose Nickol.

Table of Contents

Chapter One 1
Chapter Two 7
Chapter Three 12
Chapter Four 18
Chapter Five 24
Chapter Six 32
Chapter Seven 38
Chapter Eight 41
Chapter Nine 47
Chapter Ten 52
Chapter Eleven 58
Chapter Twelve 61
Chapter Thirteen 67
Chapter Fourteen 71
Epilogue 76

Chapter One

Lorraine Quick had spent years lost in her head. The voices, the memories. What was real? What was delusion? She had no idea anymore. They said you had to hit rock bottom before you finally gave in, and she had. She hadn't even known her name when they found her. Between the cancer and the drugs, the person she had been was gone.

Now she was starting over. A new life at the age of fifty. She was beginning again, like a phoenix rising from the ashes. She'd burned and come back stronger.

She'd spent years in that place learning to live again. Learning how to be Lorraine and not the person she'd been before. That person no longer existed. Everything was new. New name, new look, new life. If anyone cared to look, it was all there—school records, previous job history, heck she even had a credit score, but none of it was true. Everything belonged to Lorraine Quick, a person who had been created from the chaos.

As far as anyone knew, the person she'd been before was gone. No one she'd known knew Lorraine. That life was gone.

Taking a deep breath, she opened the door. Her first day at work. The first day of her new life. She could do this. She'd practiced with her doctors. So many doctors. They were the only ones that knew her true story, and even they didn't know everything. No one did.

She'd dressed the part in the clothes they'd given her. A slim black pencil skirt. A crisp white button-down blouse. Black stiletto heels. Her long black hair was pulled back in a professional-looking French braid. She looked every bit the part. No one would be able to tell she was shaking inside. That's how she felt, like this was all a role she was playing. She'd play this game during the day, and at night? Well, at night she would survive the demons that still lived in her head.

She took a deep breath, plastered a smile on her face, and stepped into the office. "Hi! I'm Lorraine Quick. The agency sent me to fill the receptionist position," she told the person sitting at the desk.

"Great. There's been a change in plans, though. You're needed elsewhere."

"Oh, okay." Lorraine turned to leave. They had told her this might happen. Businesses often found cheaper options and canceled at the last minute.

"Wait. I didn't explain that very well. We still want you here. Only now you'll be acting as administrative assistant to Mr. Collins. Follow me."

Lorraine followed the woman as she wound through the halls and corridors. She'd never remember how to get through this labyrinth. Where were they going?

Finally, they came to a set of large doors. "This is Mr. Collins's office. He should be in shortly." She pointed to a large desk, and indicated for Lorraine to take a seat.

Okay, Lorraine thought to herself. She could handle this. They'd told her to be prepared for everything. She had spent weeks learning the computer system, and months training for this job. She could handle it. She was a professional now.

"Human resources set you up with a password. Go ahead and log in. I'll get you started, then I need to go back up front. I'm Hilary. I'll give you my extension, and you can call with any questions."

"Thank you, Hilary, that would be very helpful." Hilary looked to be about thirty, twenty years younger than Lorraine. She didn't feel like she was that much older, though. She felt a lot younger. But now was no time to deal with that. Now she had to act like the adult she was supposed to be.

"Mr. Collins should be in shortly. I have to get back. Call me if you need anything." With that, she left Lorraine alone.

The phone rang, and she grabbed it. "Jared Collins's office. How may I help you?" Her training kicked in automatically.

"Hey, Lori, it's Hilary. Mr. Collins is on his way back. I thought I'd warn you." Lorraine heard her greeting someone coming in as she hung up.

Before she could set the phone back in the cradle, the doors opened and in strode the most beautiful human being she'd ever seen. He was so gorgeous it took her breath away.

"Good morning. You must be the girl the temp agency sent. I'm Jared Collins. Welcome to Stonebrook International. I assume you've been briefed by the agency."

"Yes Sir. They trained me for the receptionist position, but I feel confident I can learn whatever you need me to." She stood to shake his extended hand.

His hand was large and engulfed her smaller one when they shook. Why did his touch send a jolt of electricity through her entire body?

She raised her eyes enough to notice he was perfectly groomed, not a hair out of place. He had thick black hair with just a hint of graying at the temples. She guessed he was at least ten years younger than her, and very much out of her league.

His suit fit him perfectly, molded to him. It had to be designer. Not that she knew much about these things, but there was no way that came off the rack from goodwill, like her clothes.

She knew she looked the part, but she was starting to feel out of her element. All the training and practice in the world could not have prepared her for the impact this man had on her.

"Very well, Ms. Quick. If you would give me ten minutes, then meet me in the conference room with your laptop and a tablet."

Lorraine nodded. She was going to have to call Hilary to get directions. Maybe they had a roadmap of this place somewhere.

JARED COLLINS HAD NOT expected what he found when he opened his office door. Very little surprised him. The woman was stunning, slender with curves in all the right places. He'd love to strip that blouse and skirt off of her, and see what she wore underneath. He'd bet it wasn't plain white granny panties. Even if it was, she'd look amazing in them. She'd look even more amazing in his shirt and nothing else. Her hair was just long enough to wrap around his hand. Her plump lips would frame his cock perfectly. The thing that got him the most was the submission she displayed. When she'd called him Sir, his cock had jumped.

He could see her bent over his desk, that black skirt around her ankles. He'd leave her heels on. They were perfection. He wondered if she would play the games he liked. Would he get the chance to find out?

LITTE GIRL LOST 5

When his last admin had quit without notice, he'd assigned the task of replacing her to human resources. He didn't have time to deal with finding someone new.

He sat at his desk, and opened the folder that had been placed there. Lorraine Quick, age fifty. She did not look nearly that old. Her background was just a little too perfect. She had all the requirements needed, obviously, but something felt off. He glanced over the paperwork quickly, before setting it aside to pursue more thoroughly later. Now he had other matters to be concerned with.

He'd taken over from his father several years ago when he'd returned home from serving in the Marines. He hadn't planned on returning to the company, but in the ten years he'd been away, his father's health had declined, and the board had run the business into the ground.

He was tough, because he needed to be. He couldn't afford to show weakness. The slightest crack was a sign of vulnerability, and he couldn't afford to show that, not with the vultures still circling.

He'd been fighting for the last few years, and the books were finally out of the red. The company was flourishing, and there were those that were not that happy about it. Fuck them! This was his heritage, his life, and he would not let the bloodsuckers take it.

Glancing down at the expensive watch on his wrist, he saw it was time. The board was waiting, and lateness was a shortcoming he would not display. Eventually, they would get tired and give up the fight, but for now, the battle was on.

His long legs ate up the carpet quickly as he made his way to the meeting. He opened the door, and purposefully made his way to the head of the table. There she was, to his right, exactly where she belonged. What was Sanders doing so close to her? That wouldn't do. He needed to put an end to this right now.

He cleared his throat. "Good morning everyone. If we could get started. As you can see by your agenda, we have several matters to get through today."

He remained standing until everyone was settled, then he took his chair, and gestured to Lorraine. To her credit, the agenda opened on the screen at the end of the table, and the first item was highlighted. She could either read his mind or... and this was more likely. Hilary had briefed her quickly before he'd arrived. Either way, they were perfectly in sync, as if they'd worked together for months, instead of just meeting.

Chapter Two

Lorraine locked the door behind her, and kicked off her shoes. She wiggled her toes in the carpet, relieved to be free of the heels. The blouse and skirt followed, and fell to the floor as she freed her breasts from the bra, and grabbed her sleep shirt.

A quick text to her counselor to check in, and she was ready for dinner. She found a frozen meal, and set it in the microwave to cook. Her efficiency apartment was small, but had more than enough room for a single woman living alone.

She removed her dinner, and set it on the small table beside the fold-out couch that would become her bed later. She grabbed her ereader, and opened it to the next page in the book she was reading. She cuddled Moo-Moo her stuffed cow, as she tucked her legs beneath her, and began to read.

Slowly, she felt herself relaxing. Soon she became lost in the story, and the hours faded away. Books were her escape. The stories gave her places to be when she had nowhere to go and no one to turn to. The characters were the family and friends she could no longer remember.

Tonight, as she read, one image stayed in her head: Jared Collins. No matter what the author described, the hero as Jared fit in all the boxes. She pictured him in the scenarios with herself as the heroine.

It was his hands that touched her when her fingers crept between her legs. His lips were on hers as the kiss was described. She fell asleep reading, and woke dreaming of her boss.

The rest of the week went by quickly. She was efficient and professional in the office, keeping her distance and doing her job.

Friday came, and she was ready for the weekend. She didn't think things had gone too bad for a first week. She'd learned her way around the office, and no longer relied on Hilary to show her everything.

She'd developed a routine, and the pieces were falling in place. She'd started shutting down her computer, and was getting ready to transfer the phone to the night service, when it rang.

"Lorraine, please come into my office." It was not unusual for Mr. Collins to need her in his office, so she ran a hand over her hair and slid her feet back into her shoes, before slipping quietly into his office.

"Yes, Sir," she murmured, quietly standing beside the door after she closed it.

"Please, have a seat." He gestured to one of the chairs in front of his desk.

She sat gracefully, smoothing her skirt as she lowered and crossing one slender ankle over the other, every bit the lady.

"I wanted to thank you for your work here this week. I know you were thrown in the deep end without a life raft, and you've performed admirably. I couldn't ask for anyone more efficient."

"Thank you, Sir." She smiled, showing the gratitude she felt.

"I just wanted to tell you that. Have a good weekend, Ms. Quick."

"You also, Sir." As she walked out the door, she couldn't help but feel she was missing something. She had the weirdest feeling there was more going on.

She gave herself a little shake and finished shutting down, making sure she had everything before walking out the door.

HE WAS AN ASS. NO EXCUSE for it. The only reason he'd called her into his office was to see her one last time. The thought of not seeing her for an entire weekend, was almost more than he could stand. He should not be thinking like this.

He had other things to consider. He couldn't start a relationship now, especially with a woman he knew nothing about. The private investigator he'd hired hadn't found anything he didn't know already.

He didn't like it. No one had a history that clean. Something was up. He was missing something. He watched her walk out of his office. The swing of her hips in those sexy shoes made him glad he was sitting behind the desk, and could hide his erection.

He couldn't be close to her without his dick reacting. There'd been more than one close call this week. Leaning over her, or having her lean over him, was torture. The responsible thing to do would be to send her back to the receptionist's desk. Limit his exposure to her as much as possible, but he couldn't do that. He couldn't stand the thought of not seeing her every day, even if it was torture. He was a man in control, and he didn't lose it for anyone, anyone but her.

He finished up his work for the day, and moved on to the next part of his evening. He'd been seeing Daphne Remington for several months now. There was nothing there, nothing. She looked pretty on his arm, and was a wet place to put his dick. That was all. She brought nothing to the game. She ran in all the right circles, and the board approved of her.

The rumors were that they would marry soon. They were wrong. Although she looked perfect, she didn't appeal to him, not the way a certain brunette did. And there wasn't a submissive bone in Daphne's body. The thought of her calling him Daddy made him gag. She would be appalled.

The only reason he kept her around was for convenience. Nothing more. She'd lasted longer than many of the others, but that didn't mean anything to him. It was easier to keep her than deal with the drama of finding someone new.

He sat in the car, waiting for his driver to escort Daphne to him. He didn't even get out anymore. At first, he'd gone to the door himself. Now it was too much trouble.

The door opened, and he got a whiff of the cloying perfume she'd drenched herself in. It was all he could do to keep from gagging. Lorraine's scent was fresh and soothing to the senses. She wore very little fragrance, and very little makeup, unlike Daphne, whose face was painted on perfectly, like the porcelain doll she was supposed to be.

"Good evening, darling." She leaned over to brush her lips against his. Not too hard, wouldn't want to mess up that makeup.

"Hello, Daphne. You look lovely as usual." He took her hand and set it on his thigh as the driver pulled away from the curb and into the late evening traffic.

"Did you remember to have your secretary send flowers, darling?" Daphne asked as they drove along.

"I've told you time and again, she's my admin, not a secretary, and she is not there to do your bidding. If you wanted flowers sent, you should have done so yourself." The pout on her lips did not affect him one bit.

The only reason she wanted him to send the flowers was that the cost would come out of his pocket. Daphne was one of the biggest gold-diggers he'd ever met. Another reason he wouldn't marry her.

They arrived at their destination, and Henri was out of the limo and helping Daphne out, while Jared took a minute to get his bearings. Tonight, they were going to a charity event for one of the hospitals in the area. His grandmother had been on the board, and was still minorly involved at the ripe old age of eighty.

She didn't get out as much as she used to, and Jared placated her by going to these functions for her. There wasn't much he wouldn't do for her. Another reason not to marry Daphne. His grandmother hated her. He wondered what she would think of Lorraine. He might have to arrange a meeting.

Chapter Three

Lorraine had made it through her first month. She was starting to get acquainted with people, and often had lunch with Hilary. She was even learning more about her mysterious boss. Hilary had told her he was dating, as Hilary called her "the Spawn of Satan", but Lorraine hadn't had the pleasure of meeting her. It would be interesting to see what type of woman interested the enigmatic man.

She had just come back from her morning break, when the internal line rang. "Spawn of Satan is on her way back," Hilary laughed as she hung up the phone.

Lorraine stifled a giggle as she plastered what she hoped was a pleasant smile on her face. The doors swung open, and in strode a woman some would consider pretty. Her blonde hair was perfectly coiffed, her nails expertly manicured, not a hair out of place.

"Hi! You must be the new girl. I'm Daphne Remington, soon to be Collins. Remember one thing and we'll get along fine." She slapped both hands on Lorraine's desk, and leaned over it, so that her face was inches from Lorraine's.

"And what would that be?" a deep voice came from behind her.

"Oh darling, hello!" Daphne gave her a dirty look, and sensuously glided to Jared. If Lorraine tried to walk like that, she'd break an ankle. She did good to balance on her heels, let alone put any hip action into it.

"I thought I'd surprise you for lunch today," she said cheerfully as she lifted her face for a kiss.

"I told you, I didn't have time to see you today, Daphne." He sounded exasperated. Was there trouble in paradise?

"Let's go into your office. We don't want to discuss this in front of the help." With a wave of her hand, Daphne dismissed Lorraine.

Jared nodded, and Lorraine could have sworn he winked at her before he opened his office door, guiding Daphne in ahead of him.

It was only a few minutes later when the door opened again. "But, darling," Daphne whined.

"I'm sorry, Daphne. You'll have to find someone else to do your bidding today. As I explained to you last night, and again this morning, I'm too busy to join you today." Jared then shut the door firmly.

Daphne stared at it a minute before she turned to Lorraine. "Don't think I don't know what you're up to. This cougar act won't work. I have my eye on you." She threw a card down on the desk. "You will call my driver and I expect him to be there when I arrive." With that, she flounced out of the office.

Not sure what to do, Lorraine made the phone call, relaying the message. She hoped she would not have to interact with Daphne very often.

"So, what did you think of the Spawn of Satan?" Hilary asked at lunch later that day.

"I can see why you call her that," Lorraine answered carefully. If this woman was going to be her boss's wife, she needed to be careful what she said. She couldn't afford to lose this job, and talking bad about his fiancée would be a good way to do it.

"She's the worst. Always talking down to us, and that perfume she wears. I swear she must bathe in it. I don't know how he can stand her."

Lorraine nodded. She agreed, but didn't want to say too much. She was still feeling her way around.

"So, the weekend's coming up? What are you doing?" Hilary asked, changing the subject.

"The usual, you know, laundry, housework, all that stuff. What about you?" Lorraine answered, relieved to talk about something else.

"Not much. I was wondering if you'd like to join us Friday after work. A bunch of us usually go to one of the bars down the street for dinner. I think you already know most of the people that will be there. It'll be fun."

Lorraine thought for a minute. She could do this. Just because it was a bar, didn't mean she had to drink. Go have dinner with a few friends and relax for the evening. "Sounds like a good time. Thanks for asking me."

Hilary was waiting for Lorraine when Friday came. "Sorry I was late. Mr. Collins had one last thing for me to do."

"No worries. Most of the gang went on to get a few tables. I told them we'd be a little late. Come on."

Lorraine was surprised to see the number of people in the bar. There must have been twenty people there, several of whom she didn't know.

Hilary quickly made introductions. "Have a seat, girlfriend. What's your poison?"

"I'll just have a club soda," Lorraine answered carefully, looking at all the glasses already on the table.

Hilary left long enough to get their order from the bar before returning. "Lorraine got to meet the Spawn of Satan today. Everyone. Drink up."

There were groans and a chorus of I'm sorries from the group as everyone grabbed their drinks. Obviously, Hilary wasn't the only person who had a dislike of Daphne.

"She wanted Jared's last admin to pick up her dry cleaning. Piece of work, that one is," said the person sitting next to Lorraine.

"She thought I could do her taxes for her." Chuck from accounting shook his head. It seemed like everyone had a story about the woman, and none of them were good.

"She thinks she's the queen, but she ain't," one woman said as she leaned towards Lorraine, like she had a big secret to share. "I went to school with her. She's just a wannabe. Her daddy used to have money, but he lost it all in the stock market. It's all an illusion. Jared is too smart to fall for. Don't let her use you like she's using him. Remember, you're his admin, not her slave. You got to be polite, and that's all. She has no power over you."

Lorraine thought back to the contact she'd had with the woman, and other than a superior attitude, she hadn't really bothered her. Maybe she wasn't as bad as they all thought.

THE WEEKEND WENT TOO fast, and before she knew it, Monday was back. She was running late for the first time since she'd started working, and hoped this didn't set the tone for her day.

By the time she arrived at work, everyone else was in place, including her boss. She ran into her office, throwing her things down, and grabbing what she needed for the morning meeting. She barely had time to get to the conference room. Thankfully Hilary had everything set up, so she didn't have to worry about that too.

She slid quietly into her chair, avoiding eye contact with anyone. Of all the mornings she could have been late, why did it have to be on the morning of the monthly meeting? Now everyone in the company knew.

"Relax, we just started. You didn't miss anything. Take a minute to calm yourself," Mr. Collins said quietly in her ear, and laid one hand on her shoulder as he stood behind her, and welcomed everyone.

Lorraine took a deep breath, and opened her laptop, which had been sitting on the table in front of her seat. She'd been in such a hurry, she hadn't even thought about it. Hilary must have gotten it for her.

After the meeting, later at lunch, she thanked Hilary for setting it up. "Wasn't me. When I told Mr. Collins you'd be late, he said he'd take care of everything."

Now Lorraine felt even guiltier. He had enough to do with doing her work also, not that Hilary didn't, but the fact that he'd done made her feel even worse.

It was later that afternoon when Mr. Collins called her into his office. "Ms. Quick, have a seat." He indicated the couch along one wall, rather than one of the chairs at the front of his desk. To her surprise, he joined her.

"I wanted to find out what happened this morning. You're never late. Most times you're here early, and before I am."

Lorraine took a deep breath. "I had a panic attack. I... don't have them very often. This one was a very bad one, and by the time I got myself together..." She let her sentence trail off. She'd thought about lying, but that wouldn't accomplish anything.

"Do you have these often? Are you getting help? We have a very good EAP here, and you are welcome to use it. I realize you are still under contract with the temp agency, but I consider you one of my employees, with the same benefits and responsibilities I expect from anyone else working here."

"I have a doctor that I'm very comfortable with, and have seen for quite a while. Thank you for the offer. HR gave the pamphlet on the Employee Assistance Program, and I will use it if needed."

"That's good to know." He reached over and clasped one of her hands with his. "I'm very happy with the job you've done so far, and if you're interested, would like to buy your contract out from the agency. I'd like to offer you the position of my admin permanently."

Lorraine hadn't expected that. She'd been informed it was a possibility, although she'd understood it usually happened closer to the end of the contract.

"Thank you for your confidence, Sir. I really appreciate it, and am very happy to accept your offer."

"HR will complete the paperwork, and you will have a formal offer by the end of the day."

"Welcome to the team, Ms. Quick. I like to keep things informal, and would like to you call me Jared from now on."

"Thank you, Jared. Please, call me Lorraine or Lori."

Chapter Four

Lorraine signed the offer she'd received a few days later, and almost had another panic attack when she saw the salary she was being offered. It was considerably more than what she'd been making with the agency. She'd be able to save up and move if she wanted to. She'd be able to get a car, buy clothes somewhere other than Goodwill. So many things.

She practically skipped as she was leaving the office. She was so happy. Things were really looking up.

"What's up?" Hilary asked, when she saw the huge smile on Lorraine's face.

"It was a very good day. I'm so happy."

"Then we need to celebrate." Hilary hugged her.

"You know what? Let's go for dinner." With the huge raise she was receiving, she could let loose on her budget a little.

"That sounds a lot better than the frozen dinner I was planning."

"Same here, girlfriend." They high-fived, laughing as they left the office.

Dinner was good, and Lorraine opened up a little more to Hilary. The woman was becoming a good friend, even though she was young enough to be Lorraine's daughter.

Lorraine didn't feel fifty, she often felt much younger. Very much younger. She would often get into what her books called "little space", where she was sometimes no older than six or seven. She craved a Daddy of her own to take care of her.

She had a box she kept in her closet with toys she only played with when she was alone. She'd color and build a fort under the table, and spend the day playing and drinking out of sippy cups. Strangely, it was something one of her councilors in the center had encouraged. She hadn't told anyone about this side of herself since she'd left the center.

Watching Hilary now, she wondered if the woman was also a little? Would she be a safe person to talk to about it? How could she tell?

"I wonder if they would let us order the kids' meal?" Hilary asked, looking at the menu.

"Not very hungry?" Lorraine asked, in what she hoped was a casual voice.

"It's not only that." Hilary looked around to see if anyone was paying any attention. "I like the cups they bring to take home to drink out of, and I like the kids' food better."

Lorraine let out a sigh. "Me too. Let's do it."

The waitress didn't seem surprised when they book ordered a kids' meal with the kids' drinks.

After the food was set in front of them, they both burst into a fit of giggles. "Do you read Daddy Dom books too?" Hilary asked, once she quit laughing.

"Yeah," Lorraine answered, and pulled her ereader out of her bag to show Hilly her collection.

"Oohh, I haven't read some of these." Hilary grabbed her own device, and started making notes on some of the books Lori had that she didn't.

They nibbled at their food and discussed books, until Lori realized how late it was getting. She hated to end things, but knew she needed to get home and to bed, so she could get to work on time the next day. She didn't want to be late again.

The next day, she was sitting in Jared's office. It still felt strange to call him that, when a text came through on her phone. It was from Hilary, and all it said was SOS.

What did that mean? Did Hilary need help? Should she excuse herself and go check on her? Before she could figure out what to do, the door to Jared's office burst open, and in stormed Daphne.

"Darling, that lazy bitch you hired wasn't at her desk again! I don't know why you keep such incompetent help," she announced, before she saw Lorraine sitting at the small table in the corner of the office.

"Daphne, apologize right this moment! What is wrong with you?" Jared was standing, and across the room, before Lorraine had time to react.

"Oh, there you are! Why are you in here?" Daphne looked as confused as Lorraine felt.

"Daphne, she's my admin. She does what I tell her. What did you need?" Jared had his arms crossed against his chest and looked furious. Lorraine shrunk back in the corner, glad she wasn't the recipient of his glare.

It didn't seem to faze The Spawn of Satan though. Daphne barely reacted. "Now, darling, settle down. You don't want to show your temper in front of the help. Such a bad image to project. What must Louise think of you? Daddy would never!"

"Her name is Lorraine," Jared said through gritted teeth. "What did you need, Daphne? Lorraine and I are busy."

"Oh, pooh! What could be more important than me? You and Lorretta can finish your meeting later." She turned and waved her hand at Lorraine, like she was an insect she was shooing away.

"Daphne, her name is Lorraine. I'd appreciate it if you could try to remember." Then he turned to Lorraine. "Why don't you go on break for now. I'll call you when we can resume this." He looked exasperated.

Lorraine nodded. She was glad to escape. There was way too much tension in that room. She headed to the front desk to find Hilary and see what was up.

"Did you get my message?" Hilary asked as soon as she saw Lorraine.

"Yeah, what was the SOS for?" Lorraine leaned against Hilary's desk.

"Come to the break room. Too many ears out here." Lorraine followed her into the room, and closed the door behind them.

"SOS Spawn of Satan. I tried to warn you she was heading your way."

"Oh. Thanks. I was in a meeting with Jared, and didn't know what you meant. I appreciate the lookout, though. She makes my skin crawl."

"I know what you mean. There's a new movie out tonight. Wanna go with me?"

"That sounds like fun. I better get back to my desk now." Lorraine gave Hilary a quick hug, and they parted ways.

She got back to her desk just in time to see Daphne slam the door, and fly out of the office. All that was missing was the broom. Whatever had happened while she was gone couldn't have been good.

A few minutes later, Jared called her back into his office. "I'm sorry you had to witness that, Lori. Daphne can be a bit dramatic."

Lorraine nodded and smiled, not knowing what to say. Spawn of Satan was almost too nice of a name for her.

"What I wanted to talk to you about was the conference this weekend. I'm going to need you to come with me, and there's a function one evening you'll need to attend. I want you to take the company credit card, and find yourself something to wear. Daphne was going to attend with me, but that won't be happening now. If you're not sure what to wear, talk with Hilary. She can help you."

"Sure, I mean I will, Sir, Jared. Umm, okay." Lorraine didn't know what to say.

"Good. You can take off early tomorrow to shop, and we'll fly out on Friday. We'll be using the company jet. That's all for now."

She couldn't wait to tell Hilary what was happening.

SHOPPING WITH HILARY was more fun than Lorraine had had in a long time. She must have tried on ten dresses before she found one Hilary declared "perfect".

"Are you sure? It's a little revealing?" Lorraine turned from side to side, looking in the mirror. The dress was long and very form-fitting, not something she thought she looked good in.

"Are you kidding? Jared is going to swallow his tongue when he sees you!" Hilary adjusted the dress, so it flowed better.

"I'm not sure that's the effect I want. I need to stay professional."

"Oh, please. You know he's Hottie McHottie! What I wouldn't give to have him look at me the way he looks at you." Hilary undid the zipper, so Lorraine could take the dress off, and put her clothes back on.

"What do you mean by the way he looks at me? How does he look at me? He's too young for me." She sat to put her shoes back on.

"Girl, he watches every move you make. I've never seen him look at Spawn that way. He likes you."

"You mean like like? I don't think so. All we have is a working relationship, that's all. He's my boss." Lorraine started gathering her things to take to the register.

"He more than likes you. He's got it bad, and he's so sexy. Do you get the same Daddy vibes off of him that I do? I'd give anything to find a Daddy like him."

Lorraine chewed her lip thoughtfully. Jared Collins as a Daddy. Yes, she could see it. When she thought about it, he could very easily be a Daddy. He was caring, protective, and very easygoing. What kind of discipline would he prefer? Would he be a spanking Daddy, or a stand in the corner Daddy? Now that she saw it, she couldn't unsee it. Why hadn't she noticed before?

She went through the motions of paying and gathering her purchases, still thinking of Jared and all the ramifications of what could happen. Did she want him to be her Daddy?

"Come on, now we need to find shoes." Hilary guided her to the next store.

Chapter Five

Lorraine had never flown on a private jet before. The entire process was very different from flying commercially. No check-in, and going through security was a breeze. Being rich did have its advantages. She was sure there were downfalls too, but she couldn't see any of them right now.

Jared held her arm as they walked across the tarmac to the ramp into their plane. The wind was blowing, and more than once she'd had to grab her skirt to keep it from flying up, and showing everyone her underwear. Wouldn't that be embarrassing?

"Careful on the stairs," Jared said, and set his hands on her waist. She felt a shiver of electricity run through her veins every time he touched her.

"Thank you," she answered, and turned her head to look at him. Just then, a very strong gust of wind caught her, and threw her to the side.

It was lucky Jared had been holding her, or she would have fallen. He caught her against his chest, and lifted her into his arms, carrying her the remainder of the way.

"Thank you," she whispered, looking at the intensity of his grey eyes.

"My pleasure anytime," he replied, in that husky voice that made her want to do anything he needed. He carried her as if she weighed no more than a feather.

They stepped into the plane, and before she had a chance to look around, she heard a familiar voice screech. "Jared, what the fuck are you doing?"

He set her down, and she could hear his sigh. "Daphne, why are you here?"

He swiftly stepped between Lorraine and the screaming woman.

"You invited me." Lorraine could feel the venom in the woman's eyes as she stared right at her.

"I told you the other day that this wasn't going to work out, and I didn't want to see you anymore, Daphne. You need to go," Jared told her calmly. His voice sounded as if he was repeating something he'd said several times before.

"Oh, darling, you didn't mean that." Daphne threw her arms around Jared's neck, and tried to pull him to her.

"Daphne, I have told you every one of the numerous times you've called over the past several days that this is over. I can't see someone who behaves the way you do. I no longer want to deal with you." Jared's voice was calm and matter of fact.

Lorraine looked around, wondering if her best bet wouldn't be to turn around, head down the stairs, and right back home. They were still standing in an entry, with Jared and Daphne between her and the rest of the plane. It was either leave, or stand there and watch.

Daphne completely ignored what Jared had said, and turned her venom on Lorraine, shoving around Jared and rushing at her with her hand out to claw her. "What the fuck are you doing here?"

Jared snagged one arm around her waist and held her back. "Daphne stop! Now!"

He maneuvered around, so that once again he was between the two women, with Daphne closest to the door now, using his free arm to shove Lorraine behind him.

"Here, come out of range." Paul McKenzie was Jared's comptroller. He and Lorraine had worked on several projects together. He was a very attractive man a few years older than her own age. He didn't set off the same sparks Jared did, though, and she considered him a good friend.

Hilary had a huge crush on him, and Lorraine had seen him watching the young woman, when he thought no one was looking.

"Sit down and watch the show." Paul pulled her into a seat.

"Do they do this often?" Lorraine asked, watching Daphne struggle as Jared spoke quietly to her.

"More often than you'd think. I don't know why Jared puts up with her. I've never seen him this upset, though. This might really be the end. He might finally be done with Spawn."

Lorraine giggled. "You know about that?"

"Everyone in the office does. We all call her that behind her back. I've even heard Jared use it a few times. This will only go on for a few more minutes. The captain will come out soon and tell her she has to get off the plane. She'll scream and yell, then go call her daddy and meet us at the convention. It happens all the time."

Paul was correct. It was only a few minutes before the pilot came out of the cockpit. "Okay Ms. Remington, time to leave."

He wrapped one hand around her upper arm and started moving her towards the door.

Daphne screamed. "My father will hear about this! You'll lose your job! You can't treat me like this! You can't do this to me!"

"Will he get in trouble?" Lorraine whispered to Paul.

"Nope. Her father never does anything. He knows he has a spoiled brat on his hands." Paul had a look of amusement on his face.

"Why doesn't he do anything about her?" Lorraine watched as the pilot and Jared continued to wrestle with Daphne.

"My guess is it's easier for him to clean up her messes, rather than deal with her. One of these days, she going to do something he can't get her out of though."

A few minutes longer, and it was over. Jared was joining them, and the stewardess was closing the door. The pilot announced, "Prepare for takeoff," and the plane was hurling down the runway.

The seat Paul had pulled Lorraine into was in a grouping of four, with a small table between the two sets of facing seats.

She'd been so immersed in watching the show Daphne was putting on that she really hadn't looked around. Doing so now, she noticed that there was another grouping like the one she was sitting in, and a couple of comfortable-looking couches.

Jared dropped into the seat across from her with a sigh. "Sorry, you had to see that, Lori. Thank you for getting her out of the blast zone, Paul. I have a feeling Daphne will be back, though. Lori, I want you to stay with either myself or Paul the entire weekend. I don't want you out of our sight for any reason.

Daphne is more than a little unhinged right now, and I don't know what she's capable of."

Jared leaned across and fastened her seatbelt before doing his own. "As soon as we get in the air and stable, we'd like a round of drinks, Sandra," he said to the attendant.

"Your usual, sir?" she asked, taking her own seat.

"Mine too," Paul added, looking at Lorraine.

"I'll just have a soda water," she answered, relaxing for the first time.

"WOW!" SHE SAID, FOLLOWING Jared into the room. It was bigger than her apartment. There was a very nice sitting room with two bedrooms.

"Relax. We don't have any meetings scheduled for a while. I'm going to make a few calls. Why don't you take a nap?" Jared was removing his tie and jacket.

Lorraine nodded, and was headed towards the smaller bedroom, before Jared stopped her. "I had them put your things in here. I thought you'd be more comfortable."

"Oh, thank you." Lorraine felt like she should protest, but all her luggage was in the room, and it might be more trouble to move.

She looked around, making sure Jared was busy, before she pulled Moo-Moo out of her bag. It might have been silly bringing her stuffie to a work conference, but she couldn't leave him home all alone while she was gone.

She kicked off her shoes and ran for the bed. *It's as soft as it looks,* she thought, bouncing.

"Comfy?" Jared asked from the door with a chuckle.

"Oh!" She sat up, and wondered if her face was as red as it felt. She was still holding Moo-Moo.

He stalked into the room, not even reacting to the fact that she was holding a stuffed toy. "Stay. I just wanted to let you know I was ordering some room service, and see if you wanted anything."

He'd rolled his shirt sleeve midway up his arm, and undone the first few buttons of his shirt, giving her a good view of his tanned skin, and a sprinkling of dark chest hair.

"Here," he said, handing her the menu, so she could look.

She righted herself on the bed and sat on the edge, taking the booklet from him. He sat beside her, and she wasn't sure what to do.

"Lori, I want to apologize for what you witnessed on the plane." He slid his arm around her and gave her a quick hug.

"It wasn't your fault." She looked at the menu. "Do you really think she'd try to hurt me?"

"I don't know what Daphne's capable of. I do know I want to keep you safe. You've come to mean a lot to me, and I don't want anything to happen to you?" He lowered his head, and before she realized what was happening, his lips were on hers.

He threaded one hand into her hair, releasing it from the bun she'd put it in for the flight, and was running his finger through the long black locks, scattering the pins she'd used.

He continued the kiss, laying her back on the bed and moving over her, until her body was beneath him. She dropped Moo-Moo and lifted her hands to his shoulders, not sure whether she was pushing him away, or pulling him closer.

When her lips parted in a sigh, he thrust his tongue inside, exploring and tasting her, while grinding his crotch against hers.

"You don't know how I've dreamed of this," he whispered, lifting his head to trail kisses down her neck to the open vee of her button-down shirt.

"You've been teasing me in those tight skirts and sexy heels. Most days I sit behind my desk with the hard-on from hell. I go home to pump one off, thinking of you."

"Jared, we..."

He interrupted her before she could finish. "Don't. Don't spoil it. Just enjoy. Let me show you how good it will be between us. Let me have this. If you don't want this, don't want me, I'll let you go, but let me have this taste, this time first." He began undoing the buttons on her shirt, kissing and licking the skin as he exposed it.

All the reasons she should be stopping this ran through her mind, but she couldn't bring herself to voice any of them. What he was doing felt so good. It'd been so long. She deserved one night of happiness, didn't she?

She could deal with all the ramifications of what had happened. Just one night. She closed her eyes and let him do as he wished.

When he parted the sides of her shirt and leaned back to look at her, she couldn't help the blush that rose. She hadn't dated since before she'd left the facility, and it had been a long time since she'd been with a man—any man—let alone one she was attracted to the way she was to Jared.

Right now, nothing mattered. Nothing but him and what was happening.

"You're beautiful. I knew you would be." He cupped her breasts with both hands, flicking the nipples with his thumbs, bringing them to taut peaks beneath the silky material of her bra. Just as she was wishing there was nothing between them, he undid the front clasp, and pushed the material to the side.

He lowered his head to take one peak in his mouth, and slid one steely thigh between her legs. She couldn't help rubbing herself against him. He felt so good.

Chapter Six

Jared couldn't resist her any longer. He'd been watching and waiting for weeks. Every time he'd thought he would have a chance, something interrupted them. Nothing was going to stop him now. Her scent tantalized him. He was hard as a rock every time she was near. He needed her like he needed the breath in his body.

He couldn't worry about the future right now. All he could think about was her and this moment in time. He hadn't planned on more than a light kiss, until he felt her response. She wanted him as bad as he needed her.

She tasted light and fresh. Her skin was the softest silk under his hands. Her breasts fitted perfectly in his palms. He could feel the heat coming from her through the leg of his pants, and couldn't wait to see all of her. If this was to be the only time, he was making sure to give her everything he could.

He lifted her slightly, and pulled her shirt and bra off, throwing them to the foot of the bed, before sliding down her body, and finding the zipper on the side of her skirt. He stopped long enough the see the need in her eyes, and the small nod of consent before releasing the zipper, and pulling the skirt from her.

He stood long enough to remove his own clothing, before spreading her legs, and kneeling between them.

She threaded her hands into his hair, and pulled his head up to look into his eyes. "You don't have to," she said, her voice husky with sexual arousal and need.

"I want to. I've wanted to taste you for days. Your scent does things to me no other woman ever has. I need to please you, don't deny me this." He lowered his head and laid it on her stomach a second, before parting her labia with his fingers, and taking a big sniff.

"You're soaking. I knew you would be. Beautiful. Mine."

Lorraine closed her eyes as she felt him begin to lick and suck, driving her need higher. She couldn't help the sounds she made when he pulled her clit into his mouth, and scraped it with his teeth.

"You liked that," he murmured, lapping at the gush of fluid she'd produced. Holding her open with one hand, he moved the other to her cheeks, and found the opening hidden there, pressing one finger against her.

"Relax and let me in. I will know all of you. Maybe not tonight, but one day this body will belong to me, little girl."

She felt shivers run through her at the words little girl. Did he know? How could he? She'd never told anyone except Hilary, and she knew the woman wouldn't say anything. Maybe Hil was right, and he was a Daddy.

She let out a gasp as he pushed his finger into that spot, the one place she'd never been touched. He slid another thick digit into her, and with a thumb on her clit, began thrusting in and out.

Lorraine couldn't hold back any longer. Her body was shaking, and she screamed as the dam burst, and she came harder than she could ever remember.

She lay there panting as Jared pulled her into his arms, and cuddled her. He lay back on the bed, pulling her beside him, and arranging her head on his chest.

"You okay?" His chest rumbled with his heartbeat.

"More than okay. That was amazing." Her eyes were drifting closed, but she didn't want to miss any of this. She craved cuddles and being held, and his body was perfect. The beat of his heart beneath her cheek, the rise and fall with his breath, perfect.

He sat long enough to grab the throw at the foot of the bed, and spread it over them before settling her against him again. "Rest, I'm not done with you tonight."

"Okay, Daddy," she mumbled as her eyes closed.

LORRAINE WOKE TO THE sound of raised voices. Before she could investigate, she needed to pee. Seeing Jared's shirt on the floor, she grabbed it and used the facilities, running her hand through her hair. She hadn't had a chance to unpack her bag yet.

She was just coming out when the door burst open. "You! What are you doing here? Why? Why are you wearing his shirt?" Daphne turned and Jared was behind her, grabbing her arm. "Why is she wearing your shirt? What's going on here? Why is she here?"

"Daphne, it's time for you to go." Jared was pulling her out of the room.

Lorraine grabbed her bag and took it in the bathroom, grabbing the first thing she could, to put on. She sat on the little chair in front of the vanity and put her head in her hands. It had been such a beautiful afternoon. She'd been looking forward to spending the evening with Jared, but now she wasn't so sure.

She didn't know how long she'd sat there, before there was a soft knock on the door. "Lorraine, Lori, it's safe to come out now. She's gone."

Loraine opened the door cautiously, and Jared pulled her into his arms. "I'm sorry. I tried to get rid of her before she burst in here. She won't be back."

"How did she get into the room?" Lorraine stepped back and looked around, as if she wasn't sure it was safe.

"She conned the hotel concierge into giving her a key to surprise me. That won't be happening again. She may have a room here, and I won't be surprised if we run into her again, but she won't be getting back in here. Come on out. I had room service deliver. I'm hungry and I'm sure you are, too."

After they finished eating, Jared pulled her into his lap. "Don't let Daphne ruin what happened this afternoon. I want to get to know you better, and spend more time like that with you. Are you willing to try?"

"It sounds wonderful, but I'm scared. What if things go wrong? What if you decide you don't like me? I couldn't handle that." Her voice was quiet, and she looked down at the floor.

He tipped her chin up with one hand, so he could look into her angelic blue eyes. "No one can predict the future, but I swear I will never hurt you. You're the little girl I've been looking for. Until I met you, I thought I'd have to continue to push that part of myself back. I don't want to any longer. Let me be your Daddy."

"My little is a very important part of me. My life until now has been a mess, and I have to be very careful to keep from going back there. If I go through that again, I'm afraid I won't survive it. There's a lot about me that no one knows. I've been through some very bad things. I can't go back there." Lorraine looked down at her hands.

"I won't let anything happen to you. I know this seems sudden, but you're very special to me already. I'll do anything in my power to protect you and your little. Can you tell me a little of what happened?" He cupped her face and pulled her towards him, giving her a very sweet kiss. "Try this with me?"

Lorraine nodded. If she didn't try, she would always wonder what would have happened if she hadn't. She had to start trusting, and living the life she'd been given. This was her chance.

"I had a good life growing up. I was an only child. My mother was an only child. My grandparents doted on me, especially my grandfather. I had everything I ever wanted. To say I was spoiled was an understatement. I got married and had one son. When my grandfather died, my marriage broke up, and I got mixed up in the wrong crowd. I started taking drugs. I found out I had cancer. I self-medicated to ease the pain. I got in deep." A tear slid down her face.

"The only reason I know all of this is, because someone told me. I had a complete breakdown, and spent years in a mental institution. When they found me, I was wandering around, lost in myself. I had no idea who I was, or where I belonged. They identified me by fingerprints and found my family. None of them wanted anything to do with me. That person is gone now." She took a deep breath and looked at him. This next part was going to be hard to tell.

"They gave me a new identity. I've had years of counseling. I still see someone, and have emergency numbers to call if I freak out. I've never told anyone else this." She bit her lip. Now was the time when he'd decide she was too much work, that he couldn't handle her past.

Jared wiped the tears streaking down her face with his thumbs.

"I don't care about any of that. Go into the bedroom and wait for me. I'm going to make sure everything is locked up and be right there."

She nodded, and was sitting on the side of the bed, when he walked into the room. "I packed these hoping I'd be able to use them." He held a bottle and a pacifier in his hand. "I bought them for you, so no one has ever used them. Will you use them for me?"

Jared tucked her into bed with a bottle of warm milk. He must have had room service bring it up after he sent her to wait. She hadn't heard anything, but hadn't been listening either.

That night, nothing happened except him holding her, which was nice. It felt good to know she was cared for, and loved.

Chapter Seven

The next day, they had several meetings scheduled, and the day went smoothly. Lorraine's nerves were stressed, as she expected Daphne to show up at any minute, since they were using the hotel facilities for their scheduled events.

When the day was over, she was happy to be able to go to their room and relax. All she wanted was a long hot bath and her bed. She'd be so happy if she could build a fort, and hide with Moo-Moo for the remainder of the evening.

Jared must have sensed her mood. When they got back to the room, there was a package waiting. It was a set of footed pajamas with a zipper down the front, like a small child would wear, only adult-sized. It had different colored cows all over it.

"When? Where?" she asked excitedly, holding the fabric up to her face. "It's so soft!"

"I thought you'd be more comfortable in something like this. Will you wear it for me?"

She couldn't wait, and rushed into the bedroom to try it on. She hadn't noticed that Jared had followed her.

She rushed into the bathroom, and began to change, and ran back out to show him. "Daddy!" she yelled, as she ran right into him, grunting.

"Oops, sorry. I thought you were still in the other room. Why do you have blankets?"

"I thought we'd use the table and make a fort, and have dinner there. After all the meetings and stress today, I want a quiet evening. How about you?"

"That sounds perfect!" she answered, following him. They arranged all the blankets, and Jared called for dinner, while Lorraine added pillows and more blankets, making a comfortable nest in the fort.

While Lorraine was doing that, Jared went and put on a pair of sweatpants. When he came out bare-chested, Lorraine had to wipe her mouth to make sure she wasn't drooling. The man looked too good.

Dinner had arrived, and Lorraine was surprised to see that Jared had ordered her dinosaur-shaped chicken nuggets with French fries, and a chocolate milkshake. He had a hamburger, fries, and a strawberry shake. When he saw her questioning look, he grinned. "Daddies need relaxing times too."

They ate their dinner in the fort, and Lorraine relaxed for the first time. She still didn't think they'd seen the last of SOS, but she wasn't worried about her showing up in the room.

After dinner, Jared asked, "Do want to stay in here, or would you rather go lie in that big bed, and watch some television?"

"Can we watch some movies?"

"Sure. I'll even let you pick." Jared gathered the blankets, while Lorraine grabbed all the pillows and set them on the bed, giving them something to lean against while they watched the movies.

When Lorraine came back from using the restroom, Jared was lounging on the bed, waiting for her. He had her bottle, and Moo-Moo ready and waiting.

"How did you get warm milk?" she asked, taking the bottle from him.

"I had them bring a thermos when I ordered dinner." He pulled her, so that she was lying with her head on his chest, and held the bottle to her lips.

She fell asleep listening to the sound of his heartbeat with his arms around her. For at least that moment, it was the safest place on Earth.

JARED LAY WITH LORRAINE in his arms, and he made the decision he'd been delaying for too long. The company was out of the red, and with the majority of the board members retiring in the next few years, he could let his guard down.

Maybe, he'd found Lorraine now, because this was the time. Time for him to step back and live his life. He'd done his father and grandfather proud by bringing the company back to where it was before. Now maybe he could take time for himself.

When Lorraine had told him her story, he hadn't judged her. Everyone had a past. There were things he'd done that he wasn't proud of. She needed support, not condemnation. She needed a Daddy. She needed him, and he needed her.

If she hadn't been here with him, he'd be in the bar right now, talking to someone about something to do with his company, not relaxing and enjoying himself. He'd spent too many years thinking about nothing but the business, and now it was time to think about himself and his future.

He drifted off to sleep, wondering if Lorraine would like a house in the country away from the noise and bustle of the city.

Chapter Eight

They had several more days of meetings, and things went quietly. Surprisingly, they didn't see Daphne again, and Lorraine hoped she was gone for good. The conference was wrapping up, and tonight was the grand ball. Lorraine was nervous and excited. She checked the mirror one more time before she went into the living room, where Jared was waiting.

Jared looked hotter than any man should in a tux, and she had to stop herself from drooling. As she entered the room, he stood to meet her. "Screw it. We'll just stay here. I don't want to share you with anyone else. You look so good. You're beautiful, little one." He took her hand and twirled her around to get the full effect.

"Gorgeous, and all mine." He pulled her back into his arms and nibbled on her neck.

"I'd kiss you, but I don't want to ruin your makeup." He continued to nuzzle her skin.

"I don't care. It's just a little lipstick and I have more," she told him breathily.

He didn't hesitate to take her lips in a smoldering kiss that made her think maybe they should stay in the room.

When he let her up for air, she took a step back, and giggled.

"Come on, Mr. Keynote Speaker, you're going to be late for your own speech." Lorraine grabbed his hand and pulled him towards the door, still giggling.

Just as they opened it, Paul was standing there, ready to knock. "You two lovebirds ready, or have you decided to stay in the room and make out?"

"Don't tempt me," Jared answered, and pulled a still-giggling Lorraine into the elevator.

LORRAINE WONDERED IF anyone else was as bored as she was. First, there had been the speeches. On and on they droned. The only way she stayed awake was watching the room to see if anyone else was fighting to keep their eyes open. That and the fact that Jared's hand kept creeping up farther and farther up on her thigh. She was so glad for the table and tablecloth.

Finally, it was time for Jared to give his speech and then the dancing. She could relax. Jared finished his speech, and several people immediately surrounded him to talk. This would be the perfect time to sneak away to the restroom. She leaned over to whisper in Paul's ear, but he was busy too. What could happen in a ballroom surrounded by people? Sliding out of her seat, she looked around, quickly spotting what she needed, and joined a few other women walking that way.

"Have you known Jared very long, dear?" an older woman asked conversationally as they walked.

"Just a few months," Lorraine replied carefully.

"You two make such a cute couple. You're so much better for him than that other hussy he usually brings with him to these things. I'm so glad he got rid of her and found you."

LITTE GIRL LOST

"Thank you," Lorraine answered. They had made it to their destination, and separated to take care of business.

Lorraine washed her hands, and looked around for her new friend, but didn't see her. She must have gone on without her. Shrugging, she checked her hair in the mirror, and headed back to Jared.

There were still several people surrounding him, so she stood back, wondering what she should do. "Here, I found a table for us." Paul guided her to a table off to one side, close to the dance floor. "The great man can join us when he's done with his fans." The band started playing, and Paul pulled her up to dance.

Lorraine was having such a good time, she really wasn't paying attention to what was going on, until the music stopped.

"Would Ms. Valerie Willis, please come to the bandstand? Ms. Valerie Willis." Everyone stopped and looked around, waiting. The announcement was made several more times with no response. By then, Jared had joined them, and was standing next to her.

"There she is!" A familiar voice screeched through the speakers.

Spawn of Satan (Daphne) was standing on the stage, and pointing right at her. The world came crashing down, and she passed out.

JARED JUST BARELY CAUGHT Lorraine before she hit the floor. He lifted her in his arms and looked for a place to sit. "Here," a voice said, and a chair was pushed behind him.

He sat, cradling her in his arms, while people mumbled and chatted around them. "Someone call nine-one-one. Get an ambulance," he heard one voice.

"Here's a cool cloth." Someone shoved a wet towel into his hands.

Paul knelt down in front of them. "What do you want me to do?" he asked softly.

"Get us some room. She can't breathe with all these people around us, and find out what the fuck Daphne is up to."

Paul stood, nodding. "Everything is okay, folks. Give them some room," he announced loudly, and took a bottle of water that someone in the crowd handed him.

"Back up now. Maybe the music could start again," he yelled at the band.

"The fuck it will! Not until I get my answers." Daphne came down off the podium like a woman deranged, and headed straight for Lorraine.

"Get the fuck out of my way. That slut is not going to steal my man." She stomped across the room, shoving people out of her way as she went.

LORRAINE STARTED TO stir in Jared's arms. "What happened?" she mumbled, trying to focus her eyes.

"You fainted. Here, have a sip of water." Jared held the bottle to her mouth.

Lorraine drank, trying to remember what was going on. Before she could start, she heard the screeching voice of Daphne. It was not happy and heading her way. She shrunk into herself and buried her face in Jared's chest.

"Daphne, what the fuck are you doing?" Jared roared, and held Lorraine tighter.

"Don't you know? I'm saving you, darling. She's not who she says she is. She's been lying all this time. All she wants is your money!" Daphne started pulling at Lorraine, trying to get her away from Jared.

"Daphne stop!" Several men grabbed her flaying arms, trying to pull her back.

"She's lost her ever-loving mind." Lorraine heard many voices whisper.

"Let me at her!" For a small woman, she could really fight. Lorraine turned her head just enough to see Daphne screaming and kicking as they tried to restrain her.

"Daphne, stop!" Jared roared, and looked at Paul, who was standing next to him. Paul held out his arms, and Jared put Lorraine in them, after placing a soft kiss on her forehead. "I love you," he said, before he turned to Daphne.

The emergency medical personal had arrived by then, and Paul put Lorraine on the stretcher, so they could examine her.

"Daphne, stop," Jared said, in a firm but calm voice, trying to get through to the woman within the screaming banshee Daphne had turned into.

He stepped in front of her, trying to keep himself between her and Lorraine. Daphne broke free from the men who'd been trying to hold her, and shoved her way to Lorraine. She had her hands around Lorraine's neck, and was squeezing before anyone could stop her.

"He's mine. You hear me! He's mine you drug slut. That's right, she sold her body for drugs. She's not who she pretends to be. Lorraine Quick doesn't exist. You thought you had it buried. You can find anything with enough money. You thought you could waltz in here and get you a rich husband, didn't you, Valerie? I know. And before I get done, everyone will know who and what you are."

It took three police officers to pull Daphne off of Lorraine. They almost had to sedate her to get her to calm down. By the time they moved her, she'd created gouges in Lorraine's neck with her nails, and Lorraine ended up in the hospital, due to the wounds she'd inflicted.

Chapter Nine

Lorraine had been treated and released from the hospital, with instructions to see her own doctor as soon as possible. Jared decided that the best course of action was to go home. The conference was over, and there was no reason to stick around.

He sent someone to the hotel to pack their things, and took Lorraine straight to the plane from the medical center.

Lorraine was quiet as Jared carried her into the plane, and carefully strapped her into a seat, before joining her.

"I'll pick my things up as soon as the doctor releases me," she said quietly.

"Why would you do that?" Jared took one of her ice-cold hands, and set it on his thigh.

"I just thought..." Lorraine turned to look at him.

"If you thought anything that happened tonight would make me love you any less, you were wrong. I think I love you even more than I did before. I'd like to know more about your story, but you don't have to share that with me if you don't want to. The only thing I'm worried about is protecting you, and helping you get better. Anything that happened in the past doesn't matter. All I'm concerned with is you and our future."

Lorraine laid her head on Jared's shoulder, and closed her eyes as she felt all the tension drain from her body. Her heart had known that Jared wouldn't give up that easily, but her head had told her otherwise. Hearing him reaffirm it was what she needed to relax.

"You know you're in trouble." Jared ran one hand down her hair to stroke her arm, until he got to her hand, and threaded their fingers together.

"In trouble for what?" she asked, without lifting her head.

"Doubting us. Doubting me. I can't believe you think I'm that shallow. What you and I have together is stronger than we could ever be apart. I need you like I need air. I can't even imagine the rest of my life without you. When you are feeling better, and the doctor releases you, I'm going to convince you just how much you mean to me. Don't plan on sitting for a while." He said the last part with a chuckle.

"I love you," she whispered, and closed her eyes.

"I love you too," he answered her, and pulled a blanket over the two of them.

JARED INSISTED ON LORRAINE staying with him, at least until the doctor released her. "I need you close for a while, and I have plenty of room. There's no reason for you not to stay. We'll go to your place later, and pack what you need for a few days. Now, I just want to get you home to rest."

Jared's house was different than what Lorraine had expected. She'd thought he'd have an ultra-modern apartment, or condo close to the office downtown.

The large suburban home was beautiful. The landscaping told her how much the home was loved, and Jared was right, there was more than enough room for her. It was a house that deserved a family and a lot of love. Another reason she shouldn't be here.

"I'm sure I'll be fine. I just want to go home," Lorraine tried to protest again.

"We already had this discussion. I want you here," Jared continued, carrying her into the house.

The door opened as he approached it, and Lorraine saw an older lady waiting. "Lorraine, this is the chief cook and bottle washer here at Stonebrook Manor." He grinned at them both.

"Such airs this young man has. I'm Naomi, and I've been here since this one was in diapers. Don't let him fool you. I'm very glad to have you here, Ms. Lorraine. We'll get you healed up and right as rain, just you wait and see."

"I put the few things that arrived from the airport in the room adjacent to the master suite, Mr. Collins. Is there anything else either of you need right now?"

"No, Naomi. I'll expect dinner at the usual time. We're both exhausted from the flight and events of yesterday." Jared started walking up the stairs, still carrying Lorraine.

"I'll bring up some tea and sandwiches to hold you both over until then." With a nod, she marched off to what Lorraine assumed was the kitchen.

"She shouldn't bother to bring me anything. I'm so tired." Lorraine let her head fall on Jared's shoulder. They'd been at the hospital until early in the morning, and the plane had taken off mid-morning. They'd both been up over twenty-four hours, and she could feel it.

"You need to try to eat a little something. You haven't had anything since dinner last night." They'd served a continental breakfast of muffins and pastries on the flight, but she had been feeling nauseous, due to the pain meds, and refused anything.

Jared carried her to a large room at the end of the hall. "This is the master suite, my room," he told her, setting her down on the bed. He gestured to a door across from the bed. "Your room will be through here. It used to be my nursery, but we converted it to a guest room when I took over here, and my parents retired and moved into a smaller house. I don't expect you to spend much time in there though. I want you here, next to me." He pulled her into his arms. "Why don't you get changed into something more comfortable? I'm sure Naomi put your things away for you."

Lorraine nodded, and after he brushed a soft kiss against her lips, padded into the very inviting room. Jared was correct, and all her things were neatly folded, and set in the drawers of the dresser. She didn't know what had happened to the evening dress she'd been wearing. She hoped someone had thrown it away. They'd had to cut her out of it, and it was covered with blood. She never wanted to see it again.

She looked in the dresser, until she found the footie pajamas that Jared had gotten her. He said comfortable and these fit the bill. She didn't care what anyone thought, she just wanted to curl up and sleep for a week.

She'd just finished changing, when Jared stepped through the door that adjoined their room. He'd also changed and was wearing a pair of loose-fitting sweatpants, and nothing else. He was so sexy, and she couldn't believe he was hers.

"Come on, Naomi brought up a snack. We'll eat and then rest for a while."

Lorraine started to protest that she wasn't hungry, but when she saw the plates of finger sandwiches, cookies, and the assortment of chips, she changed her mind.

Chapter Ten

She was going to miss waking up in Jared's arms every morning. The doctor had released her to go back to all activities yesterday, and she had no excuse to stay any longer. They both needed to get back to work.

Jared did everything he could to convince her to stay with him, but she refused. "I need my clothes and other things. Maybe I can come back for the weekend."

They arrived at her place, and Jared locked the door behind them, setting her down next to the couch. "Where do you sleep?" he asked, looking around.

"This pulls out to a bed." Lorraine lifted one cushion to show him.

"It can't be very comfortable." He shook his head.

"To tell the truth, most of the time I don't bother, and just sleep on the couch. It's not bad." Lorraine sat down. Even though she'd done nothing but rest the last few days, she still felt exhausted.

Jared looked around and sat down on the couch beside her. "You need to move in with me. This is no way to live."

"I'm just fine. I have everything I need here. I can take care of myself." She let out a long sigh. "Really. I'm very tired. I don't want to fight. I just want to get unpacked and settle in for the night." She already had it planned in her head. As soon as she could get Jared to leave, she was putting on something comfortable and a good movie, and taking a long nap.

Jared got up, looked in the refrigerator and cabinets. "You don't have any food. What are you going to eat?"

"I'll call for takeout or something. We had a huge lunch. I'm not hungry now. I can take care of myself."

Jared could see how tired she was. The last few days had been stressful, with people from the office coming in and out to check on her. Maybe she did need a few hours to herself.

"If you're sure, I'll go. I'll only be a phone call away, though. You promise to call me if you need anything. Anything at all."

"I'll be fine." He leaned down and swept a soft kiss against her lips. "Lock the door behind me."

She stood and followed him to the door. She was sure he stood there until he heard the lock engage.

JARED DIDN'T FEEL COMFORTABLE leaving Lorraine for long, so he ran a few errands before stopping to get them both something to eat. There was no way she was going to spend the night alone.

Daphne had been booked and released, and had promised retribution. They hadn't heard anything from her, but Jared knew that wouldn't last. He wished he could figure out a way to get her to leave them alone for good.

He stopped and stocked up on groceries before returning. She could have takeout if she wanted it, but he was going to make sure she had other choices if she wanted them.

He knocked softly on her door, not wanting to startle her.

"Yes." She opened the door, looking like she'd just woken up.

"Did you even check to see who it was before you opened?" Jared pushed his way in.

"What? Yes. I looked through the peephole," she lied, crossing her fingers behind her back. She'd figured it was him, anyway. No one else ever visited.

"Little girls who lie to their Daddies get their bottom warmed."

"What!" she said, outraged this time. She needed to develop a better vocabulary.

"You heard me." He sat down on the couch, and pulled her to him.

"But. Wait. Can't we talk about this?"

"Nothing to talk about. Little girls should always tell the truth." He draped her over his lap, and lifted the long t-shirt she was wearing. Then he pulled her panties down, baring her bottom.

"Wait. Stop."

He laid one large hand on her bottom, just holding it there. "Do you think I'm going to harm you?"

"No! I know you won't hurt me, Daddy," she answered, her breath shaky.

"Isn't this why little girls want a Daddy? Someone, to correct them when they do wrong?"

"Yeah, I guess. It's just that... I don't want to be spanked." She craned her head, trying to look at him, but couldn't see through her hair hanging all over her face.

"No one wants to be spanked," he chuckled. "I'll go easy on you this one time. For tonight, it will be a count of ten. Be warned though, every time I catch you not telling the truth, the count will go up."

LITTE GIRL LOST 55

He didn't say anything more, just started pounding on her ass. At least that's what it felt like. "Ouch, owie, stop. I won't lie again, Daddy. Your hand is hard. It hurts. I promise I won't do it again," she cried, as he peppered smacks all over her bottom.

She wasn't sobbing, though there were tears streaking her face when he stopped.

"That wasn't so bad, was it?"

"It wasn't your bottom." She pouted when he sat her up, and wiped her tears with his thumbs.

"Your skin isn't even red, just a light pink. Next time will be worse." He pulled her close, until her head was resting on his shoulder, crooning to her, and rocking her.

Lorraine sighed and closed her eyes. This part was nice. She felt safe and cared for in his arms.

"Why did you come back?" she asked, looking into his grey eyes.

"You didn't think I was going to let you stay alone, did you?"

"I've done it before. I would have been okay." She pulled her bottom lip between her teeth.

"I know you'd be okay. Do you want me to leave?"

She shook her head. She really didn't.

"That's what I thought. You go and get the sheets and blankets for this, while I figure out how to set this contraption up."

Working together, it only took them a few minutes to set up the bed and get it made.

Jared removed his shirt and kicked off his shoes. He took up most of the space, and his feet hung off the end, even with him partially sitting.

"That doesn't look very comfortable." Lorraine stood at the foot of the pullout, not sure how it was going to work.

"If you're with me, it'll be fine." He pulled her down on top of him.

"Oh!" she let out, as she landed on top of him.

"Yeah, this is better." He threaded his hands through her hair, and pulled her mouth down to his. He ran his hands down her back, and gathered the hem of her shirt in his hands, pulling it over her head. Only stopping the kiss long enough to remove it.

"I've been wanting to do this for days," he murmured against her skin, leaving little kisses and bites as he made his way down her skin to take one nipple in his mouth.

"It was torture these last few nights, holding you and not being able to do more. You don't know how badly I've wanted you."

"I do. I wanted you too. I thought you were done with me, when you didn't seem to need me anymore," she whispered, as if she'd been scared to say it out loud.

"I will never not want you. You're mine. My little girl, my mate, my better half, and I hope someday my wife."

She lifted her head, staring at him. "Are you asking me...?"

"Not yet. Yes, I want to marry you, when you're ready. I don't think you're ready yet. One day very soon I will. I'm not letting you go." He moved back to her lips, and kissed her until they were both breathless.

He grabbed her bottom, and lifted her until she was straddling him. "Reach down and put me inside you." He palmed both her breasts, rubbing the little points to hard nubbins.

"I'm not sure," she panted, moving restlessly.

Sliding one hand between them, he fitted his cock to her opening, and eased her down with his hands on her hips.

"Now ride me." Using his hands still on her hips, he lifted her up and down, showing her what he wanted.

Once she was moving on her own, he again put one hand between them, and using two fingers, he began rubbing her little clit until it was erect, and he could feel her juices coating him.

"That's it." He grinned as she found her rhythm and began moving faster and faster.

"Oh, oh, I'm going to come. Ohh!" she screamed, as the orgasm came over her.

"Yes!" he yelled as he flipped them over her, and began pounding into her until he found his own release.

Jared collapsed on top of her, and they both lay there, catching their breath for a few minutes.

"That was amazing. It felt like the Earth moved," Lorraine said, once she could breathe again.

"I think we broke your couch. Jared moved off of her and stood up to check. "I'm going to have to buy you a new one." He pulled her up, so she could see.

"Daddy!" She giggled. "I guess we're going back to your place."

"Get dressed, brat! We'll figure this mess out tomorrow."

Chapter Eleven

It was over a week later, and they still hadn't done anything about her bed. She was basically living with Jared. It was kind of nice. They rode to work and back together every day. There hadn't been any signs of Daphne, and Lorraine thought maybe she'd given up.

As they were leaving work, Lorraine turned to Jared. "Can we go by my place? I need to pick up a few things."

"Sure. I wish I could convince you to move in with me." It wasn't the first time he'd asked. He'd been bringing it up several times a day. It took everything she had to tell him no.

She'd finally gotten comfortable living on her own, and wanted more of that. She also wanted more with Jared. There were times she was so torn, she didn't know what she wanted.

"I told you I'd think about it. Please stop badgering me. I need time," she implored, trying to make him understand.

"I guess." Great, now he was going to be mulish. Maybe she'd stay in her place tonight, broken couch and all.

They arrived at her place, and Jared's phone rang as she was getting out. "You don't need to come up. I'll only be a few minutes." *If I come back at all.* She carefully shut the door and ran into her building.

While she rode the elevator up to her floor, she debated her options. Should she stay? She'd really miss Jared, and Naomi had become like a mother to her. Was she being selfish, wanting her own space? She'd worked so hard to get here.

Everything was so much better when she was with Jared. She didn't have to make any decisions. He took care of everything. That was part of the problem, though, and she didn't want to go back to that life.

That was how she'd lived in the hospital. All of her choices had been taken away, and all she could do was what she was told.

Not that Jared was that bad. He often asked her opinion, and in most things, he did give her choices. The only time he put his foot down was when she could be in danger. She could tell he loved her. What was she procrastinating for?

Without realizing it, she'd made her mind up. She could still have her independence, *and* live with Jared. He might smother her sometimes, but other times he would let her be herself. When she took her things down to the car, she was going to tell him.

JARED WATCHED AS LORRAINE entered the building, not really paying attention to the phone call. Then Paul said something that caught his attention. "Say that again," he said sharply.

"Daphne is suing Lorraine. I'm sure the judge will throw it out as frivolous, and I've already alerted our attorneys."

"How did you find this out? What could she possibly be suing her for?" Just like Daphne to pull this.

"According to the paperwork I've seen, she's trying to say that Lorraine manipulated you into dumping her, and she's claiming a loss of income as your future wife. She suing for five million dollars."

"She has to know that she won't get anywhere with that." Jared ran his hand through his hair.

"We think she's trying to discredit Lorraine and scare her. Will Lorraine know that Daphne can't go anywhere with this?" Paul sounded very concerned.

"Probably not. Crap! I need to go. Lorraine went up to the apartment to get a few things. She's probably reading the notice now. I'll call you later." Jared ended the call, and jogged up to Lorraine's building. This was all they needed.

Chapter Twelve

Lorraine looked at the envelope that had been slid under her door. What could it possibly be? It looked like a legal notice of some kind. She sat it on the table to look at after she finished packing. Everything else was just as they'd left it, broken couch and all.

She laughed at herself. Why wouldn't it be? It wasn't like the fairies were going to pop in, fix her couch, and clean her house. Giggling, she forgot about the letter, and started gathering the things she wanted to take.

The pile of things she wanted was larger than she'd expected. She sat on the bed to sort through it again, and try to find some pieces she could leave until later. It was a few minutes later; she heard her door chime. Probably Jared.

As she walked by the table to get to the door, she saw the envelope. She'd forgotten all about it.

She was opening it and starting to read it while she opened the door. She continued looking at the papers, not sure what she was reading.

"Lorraine. Come sit down, I can explain." Jared led her over to the broken bed and sat on the edge with her.

"She's suing me?" She couldn't take her eyes off the paper.

"The judge will throw it out. She won't get anything."

"Five million dollars. I'll never be able to pay that." Her voice was so soft, Jared could barely hear her.

"Lorraine. Listen. The judge will throw it out. Paul's already contacted our attorneys. You don't need to worry." Jared pulled her into his arms.

"What will people say? I can't pay five million. I can't pay fifty. Who's going to pay the lawyers?" She handed the papers to him.

"It was Paul on the phone downstairs. He's got it all taken care of, so you don't have to worry. I'm not going to let this affect you. Please, let me handle it."

Lorraine looked up at him with tears. "Why is she doing this to me?"

"Because, she's a vindictive, spiteful human being. She thinks you took me from her, when in reality, she never had me. Please, I'll take care of it. I promise." Jared brushed a soft kiss against her lips. "Is this what you wanted to take with you?" He gestured at the pile of things sitting on the small counter in the kitchen.

"Yeah." She nodded.

"Come on, let's go. Naomi will be glad to hear you've agreed to stay."

WALKING INTO WORK A couple of days later, Lorraine felt like all eyes were on her. The rumors had finally caught up with her. Jared had told her it wouldn't take long. Even Hilary was quiet, which never happened. She squared her shoulders and stood proudly. She wasn't going to let Spawn of Satan win.

"Good morning," she said coolly as she strode through the halls to her office. There were murmured responses all around her, though she didn't slow her stride, until she got to her office.

She dropped her things on her desk, and opened the door to Jared's office. He'd had an early meeting and was coming in a little later. Henri had brought her in and would be returning with Jared later.

She stepped into the office, and couldn't believe her eyes. Paperwork was scattered everywhere, the table and chairs were overturned. It looked like a tornado had struck.

She quickly closed the door and ran to her desk. "Hilary, has anyone been in Jared's office this morning?"

"Not that I know of. Why?"

"Come look."

While she was waiting for Hilary, she called Jared. He needed to know, and she wasn't sure what he would want done.

Jared's phone went to voice mail, so Lorraine left a message for him to call as soon as possible. When she looked up, Hilary was standing there.

"Don't touch anything. I just left a message for Jared." She grabbed a tissue and opened the door, not wanting to mess anything more up.

"Holy shit!" Hilary said as Lorraine closed the door.

"I'm waiting for Jared to call me back and tell me what he wants me to do."

"I'll go alert Paul and security. Do you want me to stay with you?" Hilary asked, pulling Lorraine in for a hug.

"No, I'll be okay. I think Paul is with Jared. Alerting security would be good. If you could do it from your phone, then I can keep this line open for Jared to call."

"Good idea. I wanted to say this earlier. I'm sorry about what you're going through with Spawn. I'm sure Jared will get it all taken care of. We all feel that way, and everyone here in the office supports you." Hilary hugged her again, before running off to make her calls.

Lorraine stood in the center of the office. What should she do next? Should she call the police? Why wasn't Jared calling her back? Maybe it was a good idea for Hil to try to reach Paul. She didn't know what to do.

"Hello, Valerie," a voice she didn't recognize said from behind her. They had to have come out of Jared's office. They must have been hiding in there.

She took a deep breath and turned around. "I've been looking for you for a long time, Valerie." The man standing there was a little older than herself, and dressed all in black. He had a clean-shaven face and piercing black eyes.

"Don't you remember me, Valerie? How sad. We were so close." He grabbed her arm and pulled her close. "You're going to come quietly. You wouldn't want to see any of your little friends hurt. Make one wrong move, and your little friend from earlier won't live to tell the tale. She is so young. You were that young once, Valerie, remember?" He moved slowly, appearing casual to any observers.

Lorraine hoped the terror she felt wasn't showing. She couldn't let anything happen to Hilary.

"We're going to walk out of the building and get in my car. If you fight, or try to get away, it won't help your friend." His voice had shivers running across her skin, and it wasn't the good kind.

He moved quickly, and it was all she could do to keep up. "Don't try to stall," he growled in a low voice.

LITTE GIRL LOST

Lorraine looked from side to side, but no one seemed to notice what was happening. It was still early, and most of the offices were empty.

"Keep moving!" he hissed, dragging her along.

As they got closer to leaving the building, Lorraine suddenly knew that if she let this guy take her, she would never see Jared again. She couldn't let him put her in his vehicle. She had to get away.

The closer they got to the door, the fewer chances she had to get away. She had to come up with a plan, and quick.

There was a car waiting in front of the building, and she knew she couldn't let him put her in there.

Suddenly, she found her opportunity. He had to let her go to unlock and open the car door. When he let go of her arm, she kicked off her shoes and started running.

Running as fast as she could, and screaming for help, she headed for the underground parking lot, hoping there would be some people arriving, and the guard at the gate would help her.

JARED DIDN'T EVEN WAIT for the car to stop when he saw Lorraine running. What the hell? He'd gotten her frantic message, but couldn't reach her to get any more information. Hilary hadn't been answering either.

Now she was being chased by some idiot down the street.

"Henri, try to cut them off," he yelled, as he jumped out of the car, and raced to catch her, screaming her name as he ran.

The guy chasing her was catching up, and he had to go faster. He didn't know what was going on, but it couldn't be good.

"Jared!" Lorraine screamed as she looked frantically around, after hearing his voice. She managed to get around the corner, and was now heading towards the parking garage.

Henri had the car placed, so that he could pull behind her, cutting off her assailant and Jared. Jared threw the guy up against the car, and had him pinned down, while Henri got out to help.

The guard at the entrance to the parking lot had grabbed Lorraine, and was holding her from joining them.

He heard sirens in the background, and realized someone had called for help.

What a clusterfuck.

It was only a matter of minutes before the police arrived and broke up the fight.

Chapter Thirteen

"So, tell me again why you were chasing Ms. Quick," the detective asked for the third time. They'd let Jared and Lorraine watch through the two-way glass. Lorraine was sitting on Jared's lap. He wasn't going to let go of her for a while. He'd come too close to losing her.

"Valerie, Valerie Wills. Her name is Valerie," the man insisted.

"I don't care what you call her. Her legal name is now Lorraine Quick, and I want to know why you attempted to kidnap her." The detective leaned both arms on the table, and got close to the man's face.

The man stubbornly refused to answer, again.

"Look, Timothy, this is going to go a lot easier on all of us if you cooperate." They'd run the man's fingerprints as soon as they got him to the police station, and found out he had an extensive criminal history. Now, they just had to find a way to make him talk.

Jared had suspicions that Daphne was involved in some way, but they hadn't been able to find her. The police were looking for her.

Paul was dealing with the police at the office. Josh McClure, the head of the security department, was going through the camera feed, to determine what had happened.

So far, they'd seen Daphne letting Timothy into Jared's office. They also had Daphne going through Lorraine's desk and taking the petty cash box. There wasn't a lot of money kept there, but it could be close to a thousand dollars, enough for her to be charged with theft. And Jared was going to follow through with the charges this time. Daphne's daddy wouldn't be able to get her out of this.

"Look, Timothy, we know Ms. Remington was involved. Tell us now, and I'll let the

prosecutor know you cooperated. Give yourself a chance." The detective wasn't letting up.

Timothy's shoulder's slumped. "Bitch was never going to give me the money, anyway."

Jared wondered if that was why Daphne had taken the petty cash, to pay for her dirty deeds. He knew her father had tightened the purse strings, but would have never thought her capable of something like this.

"Valerie Willis was a girl I knew years ago. We got involved because of her ex-husband. He was in my band, and of course, Valerie was there. She was a nice girl, had some troubles like the rest of us. Nothing too bad. She actually did good, considering what she was going through, the cancer and other bullshit."

"Harvey, her ex, was an asshole. Liked to use her for a punching bag. Between the pain from the cancer and the asshole, yeah... she got hooked. Hooked bad. The drugs made everything go away."

"I always wondered what happened to her. One day, she just walked off. Never heard anything more from her after that. Can I have some water?" The detective nodded, and made a call.

LITTE GIRL LOST 69

An officer brought a bottle of water in, then stepped into the room Jared and Lorraine were in. "Do you guys need anything water, coffee, soda?"

Jared looked at Lorraine, and could see the tears streaming down her face. "Some tissues and a couple of bottles of water would be good."

The officer looked at Lorraine, and nodded. "No trouble, Sir, take care of your lady here."

Jared pulled Lorraine close and rocked her. "I remember, I remember all of it. They told me it might happen, but I didn't believe them. He was a friend. You know..." She broke out in sobs then.

Jared continued to rock her, while Timothy talked on. He was telling it all. Lorraine's life story.

The detective interrupted him. "About Ms. Remington?" he prompted.

"I got a call. Said she knew a friend of mine. Offered me ten grand to play a joke on the friend. Said I wouldn't have to do much. She paid for my ticket to fly here. Met me at the airport, put me up in a swanky hotel, the whole crap. Said we had to wait for the right time.

"Then called me last night, and told me the time was now. She picked me up this morning and... well, you know the rest."

"Do you know where she's at now?"

"When I started chasing Valerie/Lorraine, she took off. She was going to drive, while I had some fun in the back. Sorry, Valerie. I guess she's probably watching from somewhere." He took a swig of the water. "I was supposed to mess her up, so no man would ever want her."

He talked a while longer, but Jared stopped paying attention. He knew enough. It was time to get Lorraine out of there.

He explained to the officer at the desk how upset Lorraine was, and that he needed to get her home to rest. She held his hand and followed him out of the station, tears still sliding down her face.

Henri had given his statement, and was waiting for Jared and Lorraine outside in the parking lot.

Lorraine was still barefoot, her heels forgotten in the mess. "Let me carry you over the rocks. When we get home, I'll check your feet, unless you want to go to the hospital now?"

"No! I just want to go home, to your house, our home." She put her arms around his neck, and her head on his shoulder as he carried her.

"Yes, baby, we'll go home." Jared kept her close on the ride, not wanting her to get too far away.

Naomi was waiting for them at the door. "Mr. Jared, you need to call the office. They didn't want to interrupt you, and left the message here."

Jared nodded, and continued carrying Lorraine to their bedroom. The office could wait. He was going to take care of his girl first.

Chapter Fourteen

Jared sat Lorraine on the vanity, while he filled the tub with warm water and bubble bath. He was sure she felt as grimy as he did. The police station had been a cold, dark place, and he was sorry Lorraine had had to experience that.

"Do you still want me?" she asked in a small voice, when he knelt down to look at her feet.

"Why wouldn't I?" he asked, running his thumb over her feet. They looked a little red, but he didn't see any scrapes or tears.

"Because of my past, what that man said," she answered in a small voice.

"Your past is part of you, and something that would never change how I feel about you. I fell in love with you, the person in front of me, not your past. We all have a past."

He picked her up, and began stripping her clothes off. He set her in the tub, then quickly undressed himself and joined her. The office could wait. If it was urgent, Paul could handle it. Lorraine needed him.

He held her in the tub until the water started to cool, and he felt her begin to relax. He picked her up and dried them both off, before putting her in the bed, and cuddling with her.

He lay with her until she was sleeping soundly, then he got up and grabbed a pair of sweatpants, before finding his phone and heading for his office.

"McKenzi," Paul answered the phone.

"It's Jared, what's up?"

"Other than a total FUBAR, not much. We went through all the video feed. Little Miss Remington was quite busy. I've sent everything over to the police station. I've canceled all the company credit cards. We're still trying to find her. The police have someone sitting outside her condo, and were going to send someone to her father's place."

"Keep me posted. I'm going to keep Lorraine here, until we know she's been caught. You can handle anything that comes up there. We need to make sure Hilary is safe, too. Can you handle that?" Jared knew Paul secretly had a thing for the younger woman, but had been afraid to follow through due to their age differences. This might be the opportunity he'd been needing, to force him to show his desire for her.

IT WAS ABOUT TWO IN the morning, Jared and Lorraine were curled up in bed sleeping soundly, when Jared heard a noise downstairs. He rolled over and grabbed a pair of sweatpants and the gun he kept locked in the nightstand drawer. He handed his phone to Lorraine. "Lock yourself in the bathroom and call the police. Do not come out for anyone but me. Unless you hear my voice saying it's okay, stay put. Do you understand?" he hissed in a whisper.

Lorraine nodded, and followed him into the ensuite. "Lock this door. Stay here! I mean it!" He gave her a quick, hard kiss and was gone.

Lorraine sat in the dark, scared to move, scared to breathe. She listened intently for several minutes, and didn't hear anything. Maybe Jared was overreacting.

Then, she heard it, the higher pitch of a female voice, and the low rumble of Jared's. She couldn't make out what they were saying though. She moved closer to the door, and pressed her ear against it, straining to make anything out.

Maybe if she opened the door, she could hear better. She wouldn't go out, and would stay where she could lock it if she needed to. Before she realized what she was doing, she was crawling to the head of the stairs, trying to hide behind the wall and listen.

"What are you doing here?" she heard Jared's deep voice ask.

"If I can't have you, no one will." Was that Spawn?

"Daphne, you don't want to do that. Let's talk about this." Jared again.

"There's nothing to talk about it's all gone. My father lost all his money and has disowned me. I don't have anything left. You, you could have saved it all. You could have helped Daddy, and I would have been your wife. You promised me. We were going to marry." Lorraine couldn't see them. Did Daphne have a gun? Where were the police? It felt like it had been a long time since she'd called.

"Daphne, I never promised you anything." Jared was very calm.

"You implied. It's the same thing."

Lorraine crawled forward a little more, just a few feet, then she would be able to see.

Jared was standing at the bottom of the stairs, and Daphne was in front of him. Lorraine saw the flashing lights approaching, and hoped Daphne didn't notice them. Who knew what she was capable of?

"You!" Daphne screamed, catching sight of Lorraine.

"Oh shit!" Lorraine scrambled to her feet, trying to run to the bathroom as Daphne pushed around Jared, and started to run up the stairs.

JARED HAD CREPT DOWN the stairs, to see Daphne standing in the middle of his living room, looking around. What did she think she was doing? Was she looking for more money?

Stuffing his gun in the back of his sweats, he cautiously approached her. Maybe he could talk to her.

"Daphne, you need to leave. The cops are coming. You're going to be arrested."

"Jared, you wouldn't do that to me." He had to keep her talking, until the police arrived. Thank God, Lorraine was safe.

Then, he heard a noise upstairs. He was going to tan her ass! Hoping Daphne didn't hear, he tried to move her back into the room, away from the stairs. What was Lorraine up to?

He saw it in her eyes, the minute Daphne saw Lorraine. Several things happened at once. Daphne shoved him and started running. There was a pounding on the door, and Naomi came out of nowhere, then clocked Daphne in the back of the head with a frying pan, knocking her out.

"Naomi!" Jared caught Daphne as she collapsed. "Answer the door, and, Lorraine, you might as well come down." He laid Daphne gently on the floor, and went to deal with the police.

Epilogue

Lorraine sat next to Jared at the bar the group from the office liked to hang out at. He'd taken everyone out for dinner and drinks to celebrate.

They were celebrating several things, Jared's retirement, his and Lorraine's wedding, the fact that Spawn of Satan had been convicted, and was going to be in jail for a long time.

The trial had taken months, and at times Lorraine had been sure Daphne would find a way to get out of it, but now that it was all over, she couldn't be happier.

She and Jared had married in a quiet ceremony. Paul standing with Jared, and Hilary was Lorraine's maid of honor.

They'd moved all her things, including the broken couch to Jared's house, and Lorraine couldn't be happier.

There had been no repercussions for Naomi, and she swore she'd do it again if she had to.

However, Jared had whaled on Lorraine's ass, until it was bright red, and she couldn't sit for a week for disobeying him. She would think twice before ignoring his commands again. Well, maybe.

The End

Don't miss out!

Visit the website below and you can sign up to receive emails whenever Rose Nickol publishes a new book. There's no charge and no obligation.

https://books2read.com/r/B-A-QFBG-OARDF

BOOKS 2 READ

Connecting independent readers to independent writers.

Also by Rose Nickol

Club de Fleurs
Club de Fleurs: Jenna

Daddies' Lost Girls
Litte Girl Lost

Standalone
Kodiak Matings Bearly Mated

Watch for more at rosenickol.com.

Milton Keynes UK
Ingram Content Group UK Ltd.
UKHW020009061124
450708UK00001B/57